DEPOSIT COLLECTION

Dear Parent:
Your child's love of reading starts here!

Every child learns to read in a different way and at his or her own speed. You can help your young reader improve and become more confident by encouraging his or her own interests and abilities. You can also guide your child's spiritual development by reading stories with biblical values and Bible stories, like I Can Read! books published by Zonderkidz. From books your child reads with you to the first books he or she reads alone, there are I Can Read! books for every stage of reading:

SHARED READING
Basic language, word repetition, and whimsical illustrations, ideal for sharing with your emergent reader.

BEGINNING READING
Short sentences, familiar words, and simple concepts for children eager to read on their own.

READING WITH HELP
Engaging stories, longer sentences, and language play for developing readers.

READING ALONE
Complex plots, challenging vocabulary, and high-interest topics for the independent reader.

ADVANCED READING
Short paragraphs, chapters, and exciting themes for the perfect bridge to chapter books.

I Can Read! books have introduced children to the joy of reading since 1957. Featuring award-winning authors and illustrators and a fabulous cast of beloved characters, I Can Read! books set the standard for beginning readers.

A lifetime of discovery begins with the magical words **"I Can Read!"**

Visit www.icanread.com for information on enriching your child's reading experience.
Visit www.zonderkidz.com for more Zonderkidz I Can Read! titles.

Do to others what you would have them do to you.
—*Matthew 7:12*

ZONDERKIDZ

The Berenstain Bears Sister Bear and the Golden Rule
Copyright © 2017 by Berenstain Publishing, Inc.
Illustrations © 2017 by Berenstain Publishing, Inc.

ISBN 978-0-310-76018-4

Requests for information should be addressed to:
Zonderkidz, 3900 Sparks Drive SE, Grand Rapids, Michigan 49546

All Scripture quotations, unless otherwise indicated, are taken from
The Holy Bible, New International Version®, NIV®. Copyright © 1973,
1978, 1984, 2011 by Biblica, Inc.® Used by permission of Zondervan. All
rights reserved worldwide. www.Zondervan.com. The "NIV" and "New
International Version" are trademarks registered in the United States
Patent and Trademark Office by Biblica, Inc.®

Zonderkidz is a trademark of Zondervan.

Editor: Annette Bourland
Design: Cindy Davis

Printed in China

17 18 19 20 21 22 23 24 /DSC/ 15 14 13 12 11 10 9 8 7 6 5 4 3 2 1

ZONDERkidz

I Can Read!

BEGINNING READING 1

The Berenstain Bears

Sister Bear and the Golden Rule

by Stan and Jan Berenstain with Mike Berenstain

It was Sister Bear's birthday.

Mama and Papa gave her

a pretty golden locket.

It had her name on it.

"It opens up," said Papa.

He showed her how to pop open the locket.

"Neat," said Sister.

"I love it."

Sister looked inside.

There were a few simple words:

"Do to others what you

would have them do to you."

"It is the Golden Rule," said Mama.

Sister looked up at the Golden Rule

that hung on the living room wall.

"What does it mean?" she asked.

"It tells you to treat others
the way you want to be treated,"
said Papa.

Papa gave Sister a big kiss.

"Your locket will remind you
to follow the Golden Rule," said Mama.

The next day, Sister showed
the locket to her friends.
They oohed and aahed.
"What's all the fuss about?"
asked a voice.

It was Queenie McBear.

Queenie was an older bear.

Sometimes she made fun of Sister.

"I am showing the kids
my new locket," said Sister.
Queenie looked at it.
Then she walked away.

That was okay with Sister.

She went back to talking to her friends

Lizzy, Millie, Anna, and Linda.

One day, a new girl came to school.

Her name was Suzy MacGrizzie.

She had thick glasses and braces.

Her clothes were a little different.

Sister Bear talked with her friends.

She did not say hi to Suzy.

Millie thought Suzy looked

a little funny.

Suzy stood by herself at recess.

She did not know anyone.

She looked sad and lonely.

"Come on!" Sister's friends called.

Sister looked back at the new girl.

"Maybe we should invite Suzy

to play with us," Sister said.

"She has weird clothes," said Anna.

"And silly pigtails," said Lizzy.

"She will find other cubs to play with."

Sister followed her friends
to play hopscotch.
Soon, she forgot Suzy.

After school, Sister got in line
for the school bus.
Suzy stood in front of Sister.
She was going to say hi to Suzy,
but Lizzy started talking.

Suzy sat in the seat behind Sister.

When the bus stopped,

Sister felt a tug on her arm.

It was Suzy.

"You dropped this," said Suzy.

She held out Sister's locket.

"Thanks!" said Sister.

Once Sister was home, Mama asked,

"How was school today?"

"Okay, I guess," said Sister.

She felt bad about how

she had treated Suzy.

Later at dinner, Sister said,
"What does the Golden
Rule really mean?"

Mama answered, "You should always treat people the way you want them to treat you."

"It means we respect everyone,

all the time," said Mama.

Sister got very quiet.

She was thinking about Suzy

and all of her friends.

The next day at school,

Sister looked around the playground.

She saw Suzy sitting alone

under a big oak tree.

"Hello!" she said. "My name is Sister Bear.

Would you like to play hopscotch?"

"Yes, I would love to!" said Suzy.

Sister started to run.

Suzy chased after her.

Sister's golden locket

was bright and shiny in the sun.

Sister Bear was happy.